Inhale, Exhale, It Is Well

Written by Melissa Ferguson

Illustrated by TullipStudio

Yorkshire Publishing

ISBN: 978-1-960810-32-8 HC

978-1-957262-84-0 PB

Inhale, Exhale, It Is Well

Copyright © 2023 by Melissa Ferguson

All rights reserved

No part of this publication may be reproduced, distributed, or transmitted in any form or by any means, including photocopying, recording, or other electronic or mechanical methods, without the prior written permission of the publisher, except in the case of brief quotations embodied in critical reviews and certain other noncommercial uses permitted by copyright law.

Illustrated by: TullipStudio

For permission requests, write to the publisher at the address below.

Yorkshire Publishing
1425 E 41st Pl
Tulsa, OK 74105
www.YorkshirePublishing.com
918.394.2665
Published in the USA
All Scripture references are taken from the English Standard Version.

To my favorite construction crew - Daniel, Luke, baby girl, my biggest supporter Sean, and the Chosen Daughters.

Do you ever wonder how God constructed you? Not just how He made you on the outside, but how He created you to be like Him on the inside?

He created life and everything good that you see, touch, hear, taste, smell, and feel in this world.

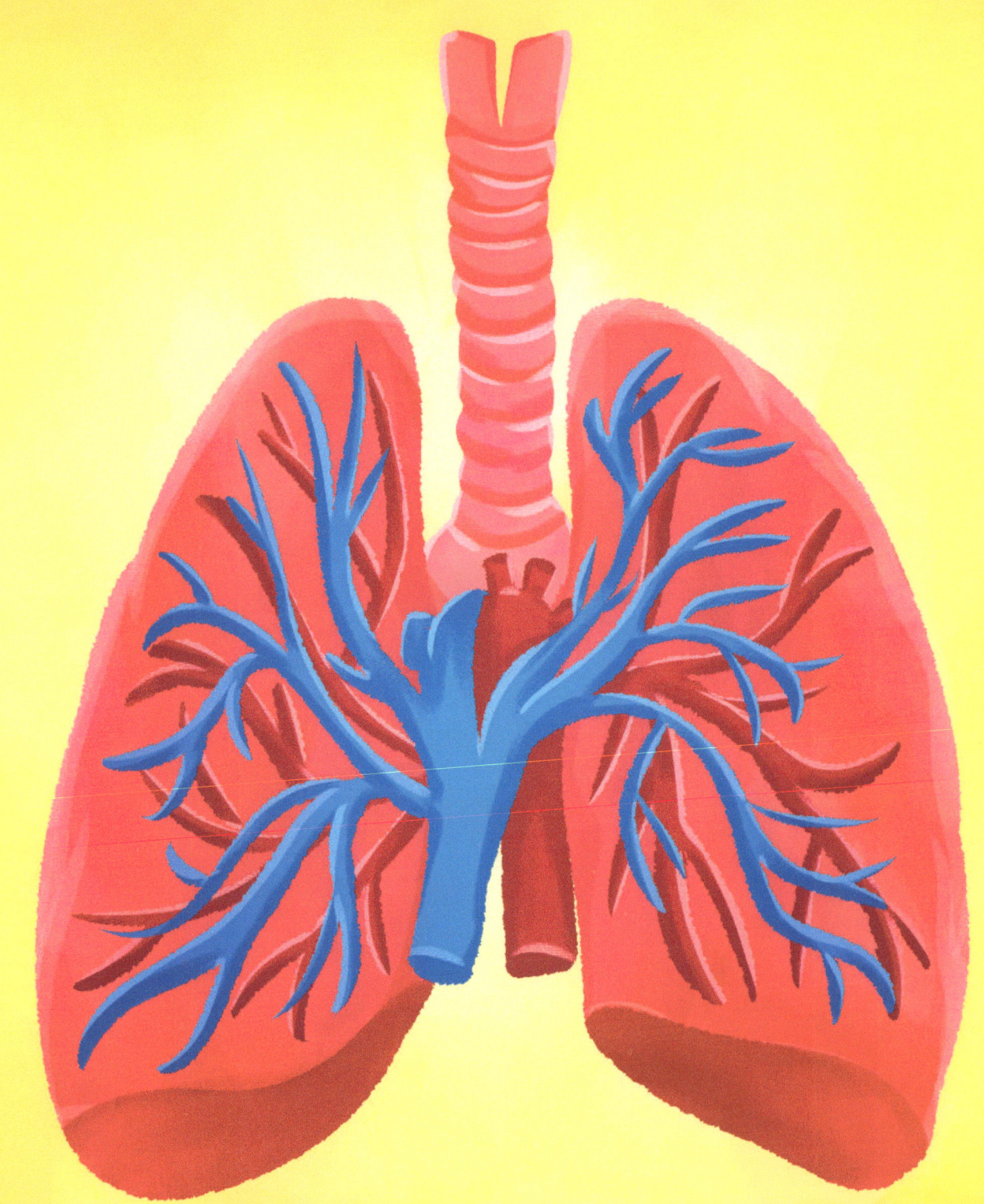

He breathed life into the world when He created it, and He breathed life into us through our lungs.

Some cool facts about our lungs:

1. Breathing and using our lungs gives us energy.
2. We breathe every day, even when we don't think about it.
3. Our lungs are like soft sponges that are safe inside our ribs.
4. Our lungs protect our heart, which is the first and last muscle we will ever use.

"For you formed my inward parts; you knitted me together in my mother's womb. I praise you, for I am fearfully and wonderfully made. Wonderful are your works; my soul knows it very well." Psalm 139:13-14

We have lots of different feelings going on inside of us, sometimes different ones at the same time!

Feelings of sadness, hatred, loneliness, silliness, happiness, anger, nervousness, and even fearfulness can creep into our hearts and minds.

These feelings are all okay to have, but we need to learn how to handle them in a healthy way.

Knowing God's love and peace help us handle these feelings. When we take care of our feelings, other people may want to know how we do it!

Have you heard the words INHALE and EXHALE? This is how God created us to breathe.

We inhale air into our lungs and then release that air by exhaling. He created us so we do this without thinking.

Sure, there are times when we can pause our breathing or can hold our breath, but we have to inhale and exhale to live.

Did you know that God breathes as well?

He breathed when
He was creating the world
Genesis 1:30-31

He breathes life into people
Genesis 2:7

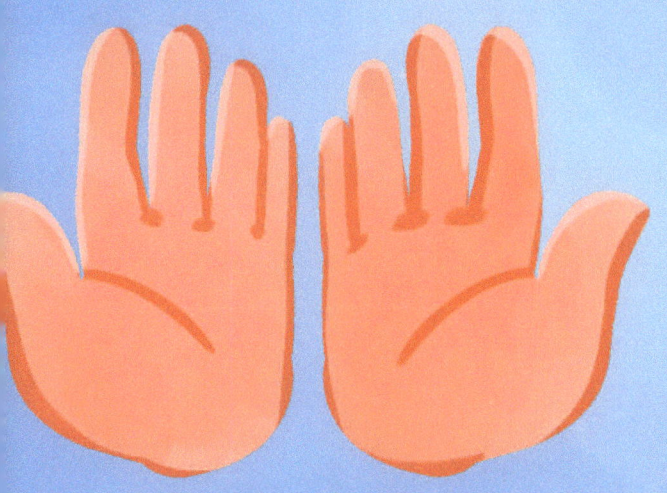

He holds us in His hands
even as He breathes
Job 12:10

His breathing keeps us alive
Job 33:4

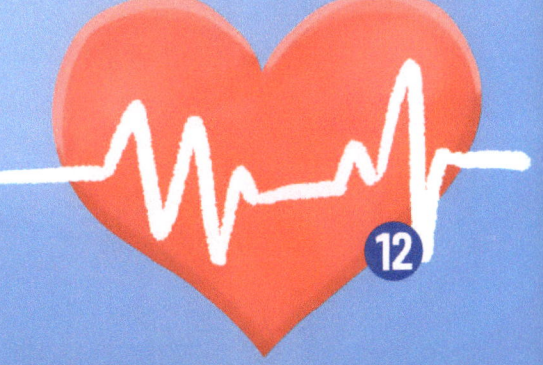

Breathing is one way to feel better and know that it is well. Whenever something hurts us or someone says unkind things; breathing is calming and relieving.

When we are excited so that we jump and run, breathing gives us the energy our muscles and brains need!

I'm going to teach you something I call the INHALE, EXHALE Practice. This is how you can do it too.

It's like blowing bubbles! We blow bubbles by taking in air (INHALE) before blowing air out (EXHALE) into a bubble. We watch them float away, letting them go (KNOW THAT *IT IS WELL*).

Bubbles carry things away in all directions, far out, up, and sometimes even low. Watch them float, bounce, pop, or disappear!

If we INHALE God's goodness, and EXHALE the bad things, they too will float away, bounce, pop, and disappear. Then, we know that *IT IS WELL*.

No matter what we are feeling, thinking, or believing about ourselves or others, we can take the time to let those things go when we sit with Him.
Then, we will learn to know it is well with our souls.

"Come to me, all who labor and are heavy laden, and I will give you rest. Take my yoke upon you, and learn from me, for I am gentle and lowly in heart, and you will find rest for your souls. For my yoke is easy, and my burden is light." Matthew 11:28-30
(These are red words in the Bible because these are words Jesus said!)

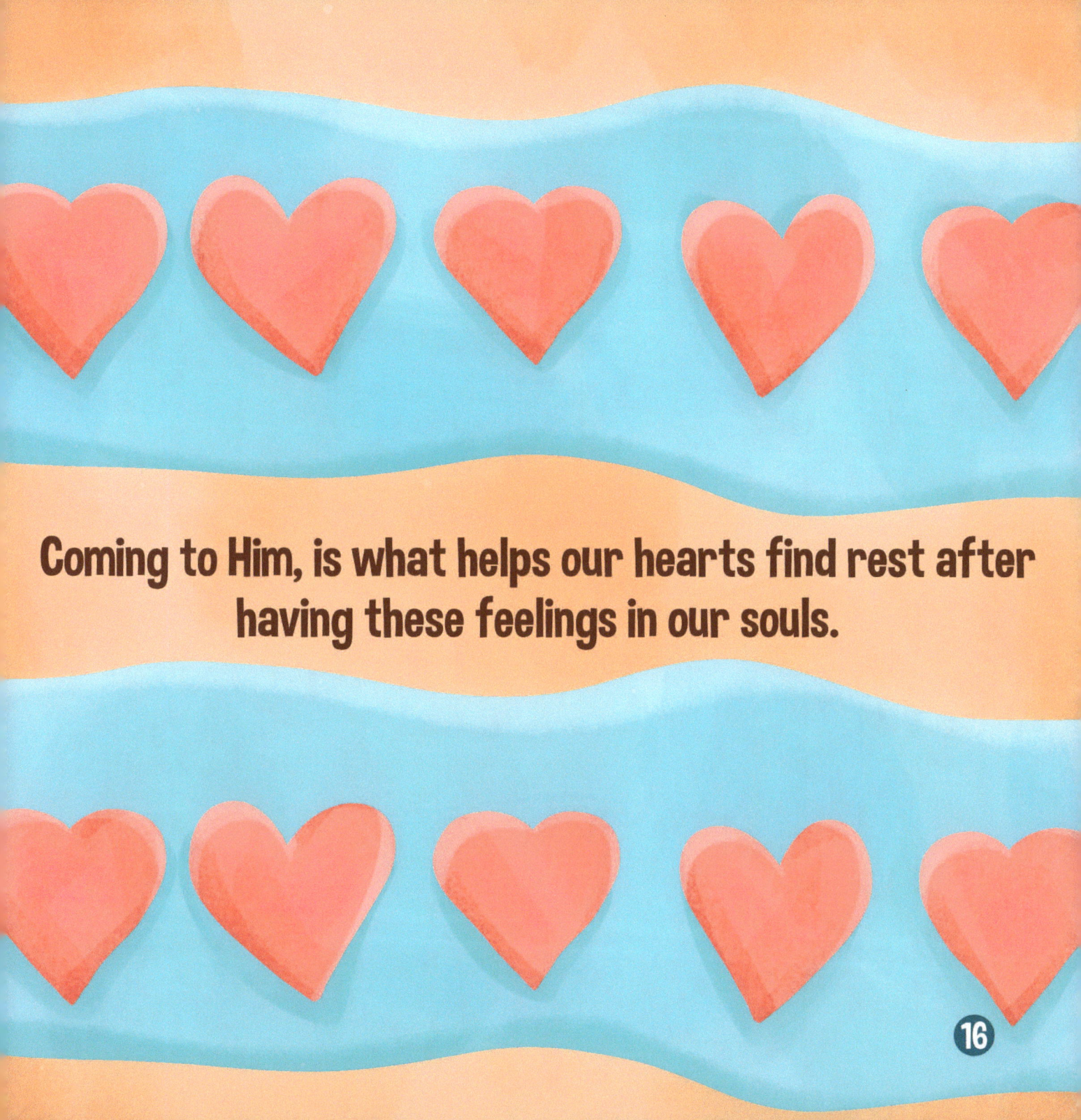

Coming to Him, is what helps our hearts find rest after having these feelings in our souls.

What are ways we can sit with Him?

Praying
Matthew 6:9-13

Spending time with Him
Matthew 19:14

Singing songs and Praising Him
Psalm 150:6

Reading about Him
Hebrews 4:12

Talking to Him
Jeremiah 33:3

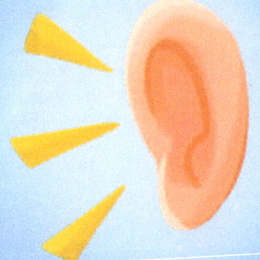

Listening to stories about Him
John 10:27

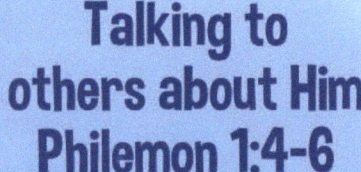

Talking to others about Him
Philemon 1:4-6

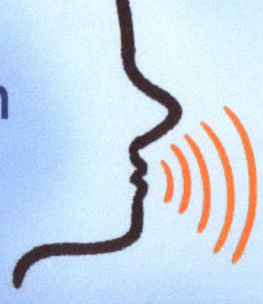

Just sitting and abiding in Him
John 8:31-32 and Psalm 46:10

When we do these things, it's like we are inhaling or getting ready to blow bubbles. When we sing with others, talk about God and spend time with Him, we get all of that good air inside of us, ready to release.

Next, we **EXHALE** and let bubbles or feelings out. We see the bubbles soar, lift, bounce, sway, and dance as we let them go. This is like what happens in our souls.

They become well and find peace and rest.

So, when life is kind of icky and you don't know what to say, OR even if everything is going okay, remember to pause and...

"INHALE, EXHALE, and know IT IS WELL."

Sit with Him and remember all those bubbles releasing. You know it will be well, and it will be okay.

"For I have learned in whatever situation I am to be content. I know how to be brought low, and I know how to abound. In any and every circumstance, I have learned the secret of facing plenty and hunger, abundance and need. I can do all things through him who strengthens me." Philippians 4:11b-13

Discussion Questions

When you feel sad or hurt, do you ever have a hard time naming those feelings?

What is your favorite way to connect with God? Is there a new way you could connect with Him based on what you read in this story?

When you think of bubbles, what do you think about? What picture do they paint in your head?

How do you feel about God being so powerful and loving that He created everything about you?

What was your favorite part of the book? How could you share that favorite part with someone?

Printed in the USA
CPSIA information can be obtained
at www.ICGtesting.com
LVHW071249010923
756301LV00006B/15